Bedtime Stories

Contents

Bedtime Stories

p

Benny the Barmy Builder

Benny was a hard-working builder, and he always did his very best. But sometimes he could be forgetful!

One morning, Benny the Builder arrived bright and early at Vicky Vet's surgery. "Benny the Builder at your service!" he announced. "I think you have a job for me to do."

"Not me, Benny," replied Vicky. "But Polly Postlady has!"

"Of course!" said Benny. "Sorry – I really shouldn't be so forgetful!"

And off he went to Polly Postlady's house. "Benny the Builder at your service!" Benny announced. "Woof!" said Benny's dog, Rocky.

"Come in," called Polly.

She took out a drawing to show Benny.

"I want you to build a Wendy house in my garden," Polly said. "It's a surprise for my grandchildren, Peter, Penny and Patty. I did this drawing to show you just how it should look."

Benny and Polly looked at the drawing together.

"The Wendy house should have two tall doors," said Polly, "one at the front and one at the back, with one small step at the back door. There should be five windows, one at either side of the front door and one on each of the other sides."

"Yes, I see," said Benny.

"And I want a nice sloping roof," said Polly, "not a flat roof!"

"Yes, I see," said Benny. "I will do my very best!"

Polly left for the post office, and Benny went out to start work. But he had barely begun when a gust of wind came along. WHOOSH! went Polly's drawing, up in the air. "WOOF!" barked Rocky, leaping up to catch it.

Oh no! The drawing got caught in the branches of a tree!

Rocky fetched the drawing but, by the time Benny got it back, it was in shreds.

"Oh dear!" moaned Benny the Builder.

"How will I build the Wendy house now?"

Benny tried to remember everything in the drawing. But he quickly got very confused!

"Was it five windows and two doors with one step?" Benny puzzled. "Or was it two windows and five doors with three steps? Was the roof flat and not sloping? Or sloping and not flat? Were the doors tall or small? Oh dear, oh dear!"

Benny decided that he would just have to do the best he could. He got to work measuring… mixing… laying bricks… sawing wood… hammering nails… fixing screws… plastering and painting… and doing his very best to make everything just right.

Late that afternoon, Polly Postlady got home from work. She couldn't wait to see what Benny had done. But, what a surprise she had! The Wendy house's roof was flat. The bottom of the house was sloping. There were two steps leading up to two doors on one side of the house and there were two floors, both different sizes. And there were two windows on one side of the house.

8

"It's all wrong!" said Polly to Benny. "How will you ever fix it in time?"

But Benny didn't have a chance to answer because, just at that moment, Polly's grandchildren arrived.

"Oooh! Look! A Wendy house!" they cried happily as they rushed towards it. "There's a door for each of us!" they all cried together.

"And we can climb right up to the roof!" said Patty.

"And slide down the other side!" said Peter.

"And there are loads of windows so it's nice and bright inside!" said Penny.

"Granny, it's the best Wendy house ever!" the children told Polly.
"It is perfect. Thank you so much!"

"Well, I think you should thank Benny the Builder," said Polly Postlady, smiling. Benny the Builder smiled too. "I just did my very best," he said.

Jimbo Comes Home

Jimbo the circus elephant was snoring away in his cage one night when he heard a strange noise. At first he thought it was part of his dream. In his dream he was walking across a hot, dusty plain while in the distance there was the sound of thunder.

All at once Jimbo was wide awake. He realised that he was in his cage after all and that what he thought was the sound of thunder was the noise of his cage on the move. Now this worried him, because the circus never moved at night. He rose to his feet and looked around. He could see men pulling on the tow bar at the front of the cage. These were strangers – it certainly wasn't Carlos his trainer! Jimbo started to bellow, "Help! Stop thief!" But it was too late. His cage was already rumbling out of the circus ground and down the road.

Eventually, the cage passed through a gate marked "Zipper's Circus" and Jimbo knew what had happened. He had been stolen by the Zipper family, his own circus family's greatest rivals! Jimbo was furious. How had the thieves got away with it? Surely someone at Ronaldo's Circus must have heard them stealing him? But Jimbo waited in vain to be rescued.

The next morning, the thieves opened up Jimbo's cage and tried to coax him out, but he stayed put. In the end, after much struggling, they managed to pull him out. Once he was out of his cage, he took the biggest drink of water he could from a bucket and soaked his new keeper! He refused to cooperate, kicked over his food, and when he appeared in the circus that night he made sure he got all the tricks wrong.

"Don't worry," said Mr Zipper to Jimbo's new trainer, "he'll just take a little while to settle down. Soon he'll forget that he was once part of Ronaldo's Circus." But Jimbo didn't forget for, as you know, an elephant never forgets.

One night, a mouse passed by his cage. "Hello," called Jimbo mournfully, for by now he was feeling very lonely, and no one had cleaned out his cage for days.

"Hello!" said the mouse. "You don't look very happy. What's the matter?" Jimbo explained how he had been stolen and wanted to escape back to his own circus. The mouse listened and then said, "I'll try to help."

So saying, he scampered off and soon he was back with a bunch of keys. Jimbo was astonished. "Easy!" said the mouse. "The keeper was asleep, so I helped myself."

Jimbo took the keys in his trunk and unlocked the door to the cage. He was free! "Thank you!" he called to the mouse, who was already scurrying away.

Jimbo's first thought was to get back to his own circus as fast as possible. However, he wanted to teach those thieves a lesson. He could hear them snoring in their caravan. He tiptoed up, as quietly as an elephant can tiptoe, and slid into the horse's harness at the front.

"Hey, what do you think you're doing?" neighed one of the horses, but Jimbo was already hauling the robbers' caravan out of the gate and down the road.

So gently did he pull the caravan that the thieves never once woke up. Eventually they reached Ronaldo's Circus. Mr Ronaldo was dumbstruck to see Jimbo pulling a caravan just like a horse! Mr Ronaldo walked over to the caravan and was astonished to see the robbers still fast asleep. He raced to the telephone and called the police, and it wasn't until they heard the police siren that the robbers woke up. By then it was too late. As they emerged from the caravan scratching and shaking their heads they were arrested on the spot and taken off to jail. "There are a few questions we would like to ask Mr Zipper regarding the theft of some other circus animals, too," said one of the police officers.

Mr Ronaldo, and Jimbo's keeper Carlos, were both delighted to see Jimbo back home again. And Jimbo was just as delighted to be back home. Then Mr Ronaldo and Carlos started whispering to each other and began walking away looking secretive. "We'll be back soon, we promise," they said to Jimbo. When they returned, they were pushing Jimbo's old cage. It had been freshly painted, there was clean, sweet-smelling straw inside, but best of all there was no lock on the door! "Now you can come and go as you please," said Carlos.

And Jimbo trumpeted long and loud with his trunk held high, which Carlos knew was his way of saying, "THANK YOU!"

Missing Mouse

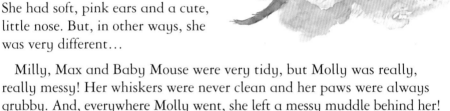

In some ways, Molly Mouse was just like her brother and sisters. She had soft, pink ears and a cute, little nose. But, in other ways, she was very different…

Milly, Max and Baby Mouse were very tidy, but Molly was really, really messy! Her whiskers were never clean and her paws were always grubby. And, everywhere Molly went, she left a messy muddle behind her!

After breakfast, Milly and Max never forgot to make their beds. Each and every morning, they threw out their old bedding and made new beds with fresh, clean hay. But Molly wasn't bothered! She just jumped out of bed and left everything in a tangled, untidy heap!

"How can you sleep in that mess?" asked Milly, her sister.

At lunch time, the rest of the family nibbled their food carefully and always cleaned up after themselves. They brushed up their crumbs and cleared away their bowls. But Molly wasn't bothered! She just munched away merrily, scattering food everywhere!

"Why do you make such a mess?" asked Daddy Mouse.

At playtime, Milly and Max would carefully scamper up cornstalks. But Molly couldn't be bothered! She rushed up the stalks so fast, that she snapped them in two and fell to the ground in a messy heap!

"Why are you so clumsy?" asked Max.

And when Max and Milly collected nuts and seeds for their tea, they always stacked them in neat, little piles. But Molly couldn't be bothered! Her heaps always toppled over.

"Why are you so untidy?" asked Milly.

Everyone was really fed up with Molly and her messy ways. "Why can't you eat properly?" said Daddy Mouse.

"Why can't you keep yourself clean and tidy?" said Mummy Mouse.

"Why can't you be quieter?" said Baby Mouse.

"Oh, Molly," groaned Milly and Max.

"I can't do anything right," Molly sniffed. "It's not fair." And, with her messy tail in her paw, she said "Goodnight" and went to bed.

But Molly had a plan. She was fed up with all the grumbling and she wasn't going to put up with it any longer! So, when Max and Milly came to bed, Molly was already fast asleep – at least, that's what they thought. Molly was really wide awake!

She waited until her brother and sister were asleep and then crept out of bed. "No one loves me," she sighed. "I think I'll go and find somewhere else to live." So, off she set!

Molly had no idea where she was going. She scurried along the hedgerow and scampered through the cornstalks. And, as the sun began to rise, she slipped out of the field and happily skipped down the lane.

"I'll show them!" she said. "Why should I stay at home to be grumbled and moaned at? I'm going to find a home where people want me."

But, as the morning went on and Molly got further and further away from home, she became very tired. She sat down by a farmyard gate. "I'm really sleepy," she said and gave a big yawn! Then Molly noticed the barn door slightly open. Inside was a warm and comfy pile of hay – perfect for a little nap! She snuggled up in the hay and fell fast, fast asleep.

Back at home, when Mummy Mouse came to wake up her little ones, Molly's bed was empty. "Where's Molly?" she asked Milly and Max.

The two little mice rubbed their eyes and looked around. "We don't know," they said. "She was here last night, fast asleep."

"Daddy! Daddy! Come quick!" called Mummy Mouse. "Our Molly's missing!" So, they searched the house, but Molly was not there. They went outside and looked through the cornfield, combed the hedgerows, searched under and over toadstools, in fact, they didn't leave a leaf unturned! They even went down the lane.

Suddenly, Milly started jumping up and down. "Look!" she squealed, pointing at the muddy path that led into the farmyard.

There, right in front of Milly, was a set of tiny mouse footprints.

Milly and Max followed the footprints across the farmyard and into the barn. And there, fast asleep in a messy pile of hay, was Molly.

"We've found her!" they shouted.

Molly slowly opened her eyes. There were bits of straw sticking to her fur, her whiskers were crumpled and her paws were muddy. "Oh, Molly!" yelled Milly and Max. "We've missed you so much."

"How can you have missed *me?*" said Molly. "I'm always such a mess!"

"You might be messy," said her mummy, "but we love you just the same!" Everyone cheered and Molly smiled – they really did love her!

And with that, they set off home.

Lizzie and the Tractor

Little Yellow the tractor came to a halt next to Lizzie the cow. The farmer leaned out of the tractor cab.

"Come on Lizzie, get up!" said the farmer. "We have the big farm show in one week. How are you going to win the Best Cow prize if you laze around all day getting plump? You're so lazy!"

"I like lying here!" said Lizzie the cow. "I have all the grass I need right here next to me. I don't even have to get up!"

"Wouldn't you like to be pride of the show, Lizzie!" wailed the farmer.

"No!" said Lizzie, as she munched on her mouthful and thought about it.

The farmer did not know what to do. All his animals won prizes except Lizzie. Perhaps they would know how to make Lizzie fit and lovely again.

He drove Little Yellow around the farm to ask their advice. Gorgeous the pig said, "She is too dull! Paint her pink with brown spots… it always works for me."

Reckless the goat said, "She eats too much grass. Get her to eat newspapers… it always works for me!"

Flash the cockerel said, "Her tail is too small. Stick lots of big bright feathers on her bottom… it always works for me!" Then Little Yellow said, "I can make Lizzie into the Best Cow again."

The animals snorted with laughter. How could a tractor do anything they could not? But the farmer just said, "Please do everything you can, Little Yellow!"

18

So Little Yellow bustled around in his barn, humming to himself and trying on all the bits and pieces that a tractor can make use of. First he put on his big bulldozer bucket and went over to Lizzie.

"Please Lizzie, move into the small field."

"Shan't!" said Lizzie, rolling on to her back.

So Little Yellow scooped her up and took her into the field in the bucket. "It's for your own good," said Little Yellow.

Then Little Yellow put on his plough and, to everyone's amazement, ploughed up the grass in the middle of the field.

Next day, Little Yellow ploughed another strip in the middle of the field, and the day after that too. The ploughed bit was getting bigger and the grassy bit was getting smaller.

Lizzie cried, "There's not enough grass left to eat! I'm getting thinner!"

Then Little Yellow put on his grass cutter. He mowed all the grass that was left. If Lizzie lay down again she would not get enough to eat. She was smaller now, and the exercise was making her coat glossy.

But the tractor was not finished. He put on his back forks and took Lizzie a bale of hay to eat but, as she rushed to eat it, he drove away, and she had to trot behind to keep up. By the end of the day she was very tired, but fit and healthy too.

By this time, Little Yellow had used nearly every tool he had! The last thing he used was a power spray to wash her down, and... Ta-ra!... there stood Lizzie, more beautiful than ever before!

Lizzie went to the show, and of course was declared Best Cow. The farmer was given a silver cup to put on his sideboard. And all thanks to Little Yellow the tractor!

The Hare and the Tortoise

Hare was the most boastful animal in the whole forest. On this fine, sunny morning, he was trotting down the forest path singing, "I'm handsome and clever and the fastest hare ever! There's no one as splendid as me!"

Mole, Mouse and Squirrel watched him from the fallen log. "Hare is so annoying," said Mole. "Someone should find a way to stop him boasting all the time!"

"I'll get him to stop!" said Squirrel and he jumped on to the path right in front of Hare. "I'm as handsome as you are, Hare," he said. "Look at my big bushy tail."

"It's not as handsome as my fluffy white tail and my long silky ears!" boasted Hare.

"Well, I'm as clever as you are!" said Mouse, hurrying out to join them. "I can dig holes under trees and store enough nuts and seeds to last all winter!"

"That's nothing!" said Hare. "In winter, I can change my coat to white, so that I can hide in the snow!"

"Now, is there anyone who thinks they can run as *fast* as me?" said Hare to the animals, who had gathered round. "Who wants a race?" No one said anything! All the animals knew that Hare was *very fast* and no one thought they could beat him. "Ha!" exclaimed Hare. "That proves it! I'm the handsomest, the cleverest *and* the fastest."

"Excuse me," said a small voice.

"Yes?" said Hare, turning around.

"I will race you," said Tortoise.

"YOU?" said Hare, in amazement. "The slowest, clumsiest animal on four legs?"

"Yes," said Tortoise, quietly. "I will race you." The other animals gasped and Hare roared with laughter.

"Will you race me to the willow tree?" Hare asked Tortoise.

"Yes," said Tortoise.

"Will you race past the willow tree, to the stream?" asked Hare.

"Yes, I will," said Tortoise.

"Will you race past the willow tree, past the stream and all the way to the old oak tree?" asked Hare.

"Of course I will," said Tortoise.

"Fine," said Hare. "We'll start at nine o'clock in the morning! We'll meet here, at the big oak tree."

"All right," said Tortoise. The other animals ran off to tell their friends the news.

The next morning, everyone had turned out to watch the big race. Some were at the starting line and others were going to the finish, to see who would get there first.

Magpie called, "Ready, steady, GO!" And Tortoise and Hare were off! Hare shot past Tortoise and, when there was no one to show off for, he slowed down just a bit. He reached the willow tree and looked behind him – Tortoise was not in sight!

"It will take him ages just to catch me," Hare thought. "I don't need to hurry. I may as well stop and rest." He sat down under the willow tree and closed his eyes. In minutes, he was fast asleep.

Meanwhile, Tortoise just plodded on. He didn't try to go faster than he could, but he didn't stop, either. He just kept going, on and on and on. The sun climbed higher in the sky and Tortoise felt hot. But he still kept going. His stubby legs were beginning to ache, but he knew he mustn't stop. Hare kept snoring under the willow tree.

Some time later, Tortoise reached Hare. First of all, Tortoise thought he should wake Hare up. Then he changed his mind. "Hare is very clever," he told himself. "He must have a reason for sleeping. He would only be cross if I woke him!" So, Tortoise left Hare sleeping and went on his way, walking slowly towards the finish line.

THE HARE AND THE TORTOISE

Later that afternoon, as the sun began to sink
and the air grew chilly, Hare awoke with a start.
"The race!" he thought. "I have to finish the race!"
He looked around to see if Tortoise was nearby.
There was no sign of him. "Hah!" said Hare.
"He still hasn't caught up with me. No need
to hurry, then."

And he trotted towards the clearing, with a
big grin on his face. When he neared the finish,
Hare could hear cheers and clapping. "They must
be able to see me coming," he thought. But, as he got closer, he saw
the real reason for all the noise and his heart sank. There was Tortoise,
crossing the line. Tortoise had won! The animals were cheering wildly.
As Hare crept up to the finishing line, the cheers turned to laughter.
His ears turned bright red and drooped with embarrassment.
Hare moped off and everyone gathered round
to congratulate Tortoise, who looked shy,
but very proud. He had proved that slow
but steady always wins the race.

Somehow
the animals
knew that they
wouldn't have to
listen to Hare's
loud, annoying
boasting any more!

Good Teamwork

I t had been raining heavily for so long on Old MacDonald's farm that even the ducks wished the sun would come out.

"I shall have to take the tractor down to the bottom meadow and see if the stream is overflowing. I can't have my sheep getting wet feet!" said the farmer one morning at breakfast.

Old MacDonald set off on the tractor, but he didn't get very far. The gateway to the farmyard had become very muddy. Brrrrm! Vrrrrm! Brrrrm! The tractor did its very best, but it was soon stuck fast in the mud!

The rain trickled off Old MacDonald's nose as he climbed down from his tractor. He shook his head when he saw the mud. "Only my old friend George can help me now," he said.

Old George the horse didn't want to go out in the rain, but he stood patiently as the farmer harnessed him to the tractor.

"Now pull, George, PULL!" he cried. Old George pulled with all his might – the tractor wouldn't budge.

"I need two horses," said Old MacDonald, and he went to fetch Tilly.

Tilly and Old George pulled as hard as they could – the tractor wouldn't move. The ducks stood in a long line, watching with interest.

"If only I had another horse," said Old MacDonald. Then, before you could say "You must be joking!" the farmer had brought out his four cows to help! He tied the cows to the tractor in front of the horses and

then Old George, Tilly, Annabel, Poppy, Heather and Emily pulled and pulled and pulled – the tractor still refused to move.

Old MacDonald was getting desperate. One by one, he called on Percy the pig, Maria the sheep, Bruce the sheepdog and his two cats, Milly and Lazy – and even Mrs MacDonald!

The rain continued to pour down. The MacDonalds and their animals tugged and pulled. But the tractor stayed exactly where it was!

The cows looked very dejected. They were sad that they hadn't been able to help.

Old MacDonald decided to have one more try. He tied everyone on to the tractor again.

Then along came Jenny the hen. "I'll help!" she clucked, and she took a very firm hold of Milly the cat's tail in her beak.

Milly howled. Lazy yowled. Bruce yelped. Maria bleated. Percy oinked. The cows mooed and the horses neighed.

Then Old MacDonald and his wife shouted above the noise of all the animals. "One, two, three, *heave*!"

And the tractor went *Squelch! Slurp! Splodge!* and rolled slowly out of the mud at last. Everyone cheered in delight and relief – and tried not to fall over in the mud!

Just at that moment, the rain stopped and a beautiful rainbow filled the sky.

"You can't beat good teamwork," beamed Old MacDonald.

"Or hens!" clucked Jenny, proudly.

A Goodnight Kiss

"It's bedtime now, Oakey," said Mum. Oakey curled up in the chair. His ears began to droop and he muttered, "Oh, that's not fair!"

"Have a drink first," smiled Mum, "then you must go."

"Five minutes more!" begged Oakey.

Mum answered, "No!"

Oakey's ears drooped and off he went. But he was back in a flash! "Where's your drink?" asked Mum. "You haven't been very long. You look scared, Oakey. Is there something wrong?"

"There's a monster in the kitchen, with long, white shaggy hair, lurking in the corner, behind the rocking chair," said Oakey.

Mum laughed. "Oh, Oakey, you've made a mistake. That's no monster. It's a mop." And she gave the mop a shake.

Oakey's ears drooped and off he went. But he was back in a flash! "What's the matter?" asked Mum.

"There's a ghost in the hallway, hovering around. Look, there it is floating just above the ground," he wailed.

"Oh, Oakey, you've made a mistake. That's no ghost. It's just an old coat, hanging on the hook. Coats don't float!" laughed Mum.

A GOODNIGHT KISS

Oakey's ears drooped and off he went. But he was back in a flash! "Why aren't you in bed, Oakey?" asked Mum.

"There's a great big lump beneath the sheets. It's waiting to get me. I'm scared it's going to pounce. Please come and see," sniffed Oakey.

"Oh, Oakey, you've made a mistake. The only thing underneath the sheets is your old teddy bear," smiled Mum.

Oakey's ears drooped and he got into bed. But he didn't close his eyes. "Why aren't you asleep?" asked Mum.

"There are huge creepy crawlies underneath my bed. And I can't get the thought of them out of my head," complained Oakey.

"They're just your slippers, Oakey, so there's no need to hide. They won't be creeping anywhere without your feet inside," grinned Mum. "That's it now, Oakey. Time to say goodnight."

Mum left the room, switching off the light. And then Oakey saw it by the door. The monster! It moved across the floor and walked straight towards him, with its arms stretched out. Oakey's mouth opened, but he found he couldn't shout. The monster leaned over him and Oakey closed his eyes. What happened next gave Oakey an enormous surprise. The monster picked him up and cuddled him tight. Monsters just don't do that.

This couldn't be right! Then Mum's voice whispered, "Don't worry, it's just me. When I said 'Goodnight' just now, I forgot to give you this." Then Monster Mum gave Oakey a goodnight kiss!

This is a Parragon Book
This edition published in 2004

Parragon
Queen Street House
4 Queen Street
Bath BA1 1HE, UK

ISBN 1-40544-210-7

Printed in Indonesia